The Great White Owl of Sissinghurst

The Great White Owl of Sissinghurst

DAWN LANGLEY SIMMONS

ILLUSTRATED BY S. D. SCHINDLER

MARGARET K. McELDERRY BOOKS
NEW YORK

MAXWELL MACMILLAN CANADA
TORONTO

MAXWELL MACMILLAN INTERNATIONAL
NEW YORK   OXFORD   SINGAPORE   SYDNEY

Margaret K. McElderry Books, Macmillan Publishing Company, 866 Third Avenue, New York, NY 10022
Maxwell Macmillan Canada, Inc., 1200 Eglinton Avenue East, Suite 200, Don Mills, Ontario M3C 3N1
Macmillan Publishing Company is part of the Maxwell Communication Group of Companies.

The text of this book is set in Usherwood Medium. The illustrations are rendered in ink with gouache.
First edition   Printed in Hong Kong by South China Publishing Company (1988) Ltd.
10 9 8 7 6 5 4 3 2 1

Library of Congress Cataloging-in-Publication Data
Simmons, Dawn Langley.   The great white owl of Sissinghurst / Dawn Langley Simmons ;
illustrated by S. D. Schindler — 1st ed.   p.   cm.
Summary: Three young children staying at an English castle are fascinated by the great white owl
that haunts the grounds and rescue it when it is shot by a hunter.
ISBN 0-689-50522-1
[1. Owls—Fiction.   2. Castles—Fiction.]   I. Schindler, S. D., ill.   II. Title.   PZ7.S5916Gr 1993
[Fic]—dc20   91-17490

For Damian Patrick Hall

—D.L.S.

To Rita, Bob, and Kitty—
my intrepid visual referencers, many thanks!

—S.D.S.

THE GREAT WHITE OWL lived under the roof over Copper's garage. He had lived there as long as anyone could remember. Copper called him King, which seemed to suit him perfectly. Copper was the caretaker of Sissinghurst Castle in England. The owners were traveling far away.

Fay and Dawn were sisters, aged seven and eight, who were visiting the castle with their six-year-old cousin David. David wore horn-rimmed spectacles and enjoyed his visits to the castle very much. They shared a room, with diamond-paned windows, up in the big red tower. The tower had two pointed turrets that looked like a pair of witches' caps, Fay said.

Each night at dusk the children stood in their nightclothes gazing out of the open window, hoping for a glimpse of King, the great white owl of Sissinghurst, as he glided ghostlike across the silent green lawns over which Elizabeth, the Tudor queen, had once walked. He glided to the White Garden, filled with sweet white roses, white lilies, and white clematis draped like giant cobwebs across the apple trees. There he spent the warm spring and summer nights.

Satisfied when they had seen their beloved King, the children went happily to sleep, Fay and Dawn in a large four-poster bed with rich hangings of crimson and gold. David, his spectacles laid carefully on a little blue-painted table, slept in a real mahogany sleigh bed that the children's grandfather had discovered in an antique shop far across the gray Atlantic Ocean in Canada.

When morning came the children awoke to the *tap-tap* made by the woodpeckers as they hunted for tiny insects in the crevices of the wooden shingles that covered the pointed turret caps. Somewhere out in Castle Woods a red fox called to its mate, and the moorhens down on the lake shrieked as they sped like miniature outboard motorboats through the choppy water.

Then the children heard the heavy *clip-clop* of Copper's black leather boots as he slowly climbed the winding staircase to wind the big tower clock and run up the flag.

The White Garden was damp with morning dew. King, the great white owl, had long since left his perch on the head of the carved lion over the grilled gateway and had returned safely to his dark daytime quarters high above the oaken beams of Copper's garage.

All day long the children played by the lake where there was a flat-bottomed boat. Sometimes, if Copper was in a good mood, he would take them for a little voyage to the island where the tall bulrushes grew. Copper had strong arms, with short orange hairs all over them. He liked to sing as he punted the flat-bottomed boat with the long single oar. He sang a rhyme that he had learned as a little boy:

> *"Adam and Eve and Pinch-Me*
> *went down to the river to bathe;*
> *Adam and Eve were drown-ded,*
> *so who do you think was saved?"*

"Pinch-Me," shouted David, and of course the girls did!

When evening came and the sun was going to bed, the children were tired of picking yellow water-lilies so Copper headed the flat-bottomed boat back to shore. There he picked up the bucket of food for the black-and-white sheep that grazed under the giant oak trees. They were called Jacob's sheep after Jacob, Joseph's elderly father in the Bible story. Some of the sheep had little woolly lambs and were so tame that they poked their heads into the tin bucket before Copper could spread the contents over the grass.

Then Copper took another bucket that had a deep dent in the side, and with the children and Nelly, his wife's spaniel, barking at his heels, he climbed the steep mossy path between the avenue of tall poplar trees to where Old Abdul the donkey was waiting patiently for his supper.

Old Abdul loved living at Sissinghurst. For years he had worked very hard in faraway Morocco, pulling a heavy cart. He had been beaten with a stick by his cruel master when his short legs grew tired, making him walk slowly. At last, Fay and Dawn's parents rescued him and he was brought on a big ship to live at the castle. There he sometimes pulled a small, bright yellow cart full of weeds from the flower beds, but not very often. Old Abdul had a very short temper and if anything displeased him he would take off at a trot, still wearing his straw bonnet, with the garden boy running behind him. Old Abdul would then kick up his legs as if he were a young donkey again and would pitch his little yellow cart, filled to the brim with brambles and stinging nettles, right into the moat!

When the children, Copper, and his wife's dog, Nelly, reached the little shed thatched with heather where Old Abdul lived, they found him outside doing what he liked best to do—smelling buttercups!

Old Abdul was pleased to see his visitors and, of course, his supper, but first he made a beeline straight for the pocket in David's shorts, for he knew that David often kept a strawberry jelly doughnut all squashed up in that pocket!

David had just given Old Abdul the squashed strawberry jelly doughnut when they heard the familiar flapping of wings. Looking up, they saw King, the great white owl of Sissinghurst, as once more he began his evening adventure.

"King!" Fay, Dawn, and David all shouted together. And King must have heard and understood them, for three beautiful snow-white feathers, one for each of them, came fluttering to the ground.

Next morning the children rose early. They had planned an expedition to the Black Hole, a deep cavernlike place, overgrown with ferns and elderberry branches. It was dark and spooky, even in broad daylight. To get there, they took the flagstone path through the White Garden. Suddenly, Fay cried out, "It's King....Somebody has killed him!"

King lay on the ground, one great wing stretched out useless...all red with blood.

"Is he *really* dead," asked David, trying to be brave and not cry.

"No," said Dawn. "Look, his eyes are blinking.

"David, run and fetch Copper. He will know what to do; he always does."

David ran as fast as his short legs would carry him to the big garage. Copper could usually be found there, working on one of the cars.

After what seemed forever to Fay and Dawn, watching over the injured white owl, David returned with Copper, whose face was red from hurrying.

Copper bent over the wounded bird, gently lifting the broken wing. "King must have flown beyond the castle boundaries," he said. "Somebody shot him and he must have struggled home before falling to the ground."

Finished, he carried the large bird back to the garage. King seemed to understand that Copper was helping him and did not struggle. Climbing the ladder, Copper placed him safely in the dark recess under the roof where King lived.

Later, Copper told David to ride on his bicycle to the village and buy two pounds of ground beef from Mr. Burgess the butcher, so that they would have plenty of food for King to eat now that he could not go out and look for his own supper.

"Of course, his broken wing may never heal," said Copper sadly. "Only time will tell."

But King's wing *did* heal, and one early evening when the green frogs were croaking loudly in the moat and the three children were preparing for bed, they suddenly heard a familiar sound!

Finished, he carried the large bird back to the garage. King seemed to understand that Copper was helping him and did not struggle. Climbing the ladder, Copper placed him safely in the dark recess under the roof where King lived.

Later, Copper told David to ride on his bicycle to the village and buy two pounds of ground beef from Mr. Burgess the butcher, so that they would have plenty of food for King to eat now that he could not go out and look for his own supper.

"Of course, his broken wing may never heal," said Copper sadly. "Only time will tell."

But King's wing *did* heal, and one early evening when the green frogs were croaking loudly in the moat and the three children were preparing for bed, they suddenly heard a familiar sound!

He lifted the great white owl into his arms and, with the children following anxiously behind, hurried home to his redbrick cottage, where he laid King carefully on top of the spotlessly clean kitchen table.

Telling the children to stand on either side to make sure that King did not fall off, Copper left them for a few minutes. He came back with a narrow branch he had cut out of a lilac bush with his pruning knife. He fashioned the branch into a splint, which he fixed to King's damaged wing.

"*Te whit to whoo . . . ! Te whit to whoo.*"

"King!" they shouted all together, rushing to the diamond-paned window just in time to see King, the great white owl of Sissinghurst, as he swooped down to his own perch on the stone lion's head in the beautiful White Garden.